P9-DDT-196
3 9048 08940095 0

OCT 11

S.S.F. Public Library
West Orange
840 West Orange Ave.
South San Francisco, CA 94080

STONE ARCH BOOKS
a capstone imprint

Sports Illustrated KIDS

I Only Surf Online

by Val Priebe

illustrated by Jorge Santillan

STONE ARCH BOOKS

a capstone imprint

Sports Illustrated KIDS *I Only Surf Online*
is published by Stone Arch Books — A Capstone Imprint
151 Good Counsel Drive, P.O. Box 669
Mankato, Minnesota 56002
www.capstonepub.com

Art Director: Bob Lentz
Graphic Designer: Hilary Wacholz
Production Specialist: Michelle Biedscheid

Timeline photo credits: Library of Congress (top right);
Shutterstock/Bruce C. Murray (top left), Igor Golovniov (middle
left), Jarvis Gray (middle right); Sports Illustrated/Robert Beck
(bottom).

Printed in the United States of America in Stevens Point, Wisconsin.
032011   006111WZF11

Copyright © 2012 by Stone Arch Books.
All rights reserved. No part of this publication may be reproduced in whole
or in part, or stored in a retrieval system, or transmitted in any form or by
any means, electronic, mechanical, photocopying, recording, or otherwise,
without written permission of the publisher, or where applicable Time Inc.
For information regarding permissions, write to Stone Arch Books, 151 Good
Counsel Drive, P.O. Box 669, Dept. R, Mankato, MN 56002. SI KIDS is a
trademark of Time Inc. Used with permission.

Library of Congress Cataloging-in-Publication Data
Priebe, Val.
I only surf online / by Val Priebe; illustrated by Jorge H. Santillan.
  p. cm. --- (Sports Illustrated kids. Victory School superstars)
Summary: Carmen takes surfing lessons while on a school trip.
ISBN 978-1-4342-2233-6 (library binding)
ISBN 978-1-4342-3394-3 (pbk.)
  1. Surfing—Juvenile fiction. 2. Persistence—Juvenile fiction. [1.
Surfing—Fiction. 2. Persistence—Fiction.] I. Santillan, Jorge, ill. II. Title. III.
Series: Sports Illustrated kids. Victory School superstars.
  PZ7.P934287Iam 2011
[Fic]—dc22   2011002304

TABLE of CONTENTS

CARMEN SKORE

Surfing

AGE: 10
GRADE: 4
SUPER SPORTS ABILITY: Super Dribbling

VICTORY SCHOOL SUPERSTARS

Playa Victoria Superstars:

JOSH   CARMEN   TYLER

Playa Victoria

Don't let Playa Victoria's relaxed vibe fool you. Here, athletes work hard as they soak up the rays. The best of the best train at this gorgeous beach resort. Learn summer sports like beach volleyball, wakeboarding, and surfing from the top experts.

1. Surf Shack
2. Volleyball Court
3. Main Boat Dock
4. Resort Lodge
5. Bungalows

A Mystery Surfer

It seems like I've been counting down the days until this school trip forever. And now here I am, walking on the beach at the sports resort, Playa Victoria. Every year the Victory school takes a trip here so we can try new water and beach sports.

Everyone that goes to Victory has a super skill. Mine is dribbling. No matter what, I will never ever lose the ball while I'm dribbling.

I probably won't be using my skill much this week. But I love trying new things, even if I'm not super at them!

We're staying in little houses on the beach while we're here. I didn't know the other girls in my cabin very well, but they're all really nice.

I made friends with Sarah almost right away. We decided to take surfing lessons while we are here.

Sarah is a gymnast. Her super skill is balance. She never falls off the balance beam!

As we walk to dinner, Sarah is walking on her hands just as easily as I walk on my feet. I shake my head and say, "Try not to eat any sand, Sarah! You'll ruin your dinner."

Looking out at the ocean, I notice a surfer riding a huge wave. I can't see her face, but I can tell she's a girl.

She's floating along the top of the water. The wave she is riding is monstrous, but she doesn't seem scared at all! I have never seen anything like it. Now I can't wait to surf!

"Sarah, look!" I say. "That surfer is amazing!" But the ocean is too loud, and Sarah doesn't hear me.

I tug on her leg and yell as loud as I can, "LOOK AT THAT SURFER!"

"What surfer?" Sarah asks.

She's gone!

I start to explain, but the roar of the waves on the sand is replaced by the voices in the lunchroom. My stomach growls with hunger. I stand in line behind Sarah. I can't stop thinking about surfing like that girl.

Face Full
of Water

The next day, Sarah and I hurry to the surf shack right after breakfast. There are a few other girls waiting there already. I look for the mystery surfer, but I don't see her.

"Hello, girls!" says a woman's voice. "I'm Jeanie, and I'll be your surfing instructor while you're at Playa Victoria."

It's Jeanie Sanchez! Last year, my dad and I went to Mexico to visit my grandparents. My grandma showed me a scrapbook Dad made when he was young. There was a picture of Jeanie from a newspaper. Grandma told me she was the best surfer in Mexico.

We learn how to pick out a surfboard
and walk to the water. I have to pick
a shorter board because I'm not very
tall. Sarah's is a little longer. One girl I
recognize from the volleyball team picks
the longest board of all.

"Boards in the water!" says Jeanie. "Now lay on your board on your stomach and practice paddling with your arms. Make sure the front of your board doesn't go underwater."

I try to do what Jeanie says, but my board goes right under. I get a face full of water.

Surfing is going to be harder than I thought! I am also having a hard time focusing. I keep thinking about that mystery surfer and how easy surfing looked.

After a while, we try to stand up on our boards. Of course, Sarah doesn't have any problems. But the waves make me lose my balance over and over.

"Carmen," I hear Jeanie say, "you're a basketball player, right?"

"Yes," I say. *What does basketball have to do with surfing*? I wonder.

"When you stand up, keep your knees bent," says Jeanie. "Just like you're playing defense."

I try it. I stand up on my board for a few seconds longer than before until . . . *SPLASH!* I fall into the water again.

Suddenly, I have a sinking feeling. I usually like trying new things. But I am not having fun surfing. To make matters worse, I can see Sarah standing on her board. She makes it look so easy!

After our lesson, we are gathering our things when Sarah points toward the ocean. "Carmen, is that the surfer you were talking about last night?" she asks.

I look where Sarah is pointing. There she is! As we watch, she rides a huge wave all the way into the beach. Without missing a beat, she walks off of her surfboard and onto the sand.

"Whoa!" says Sarah.

"That was amazing!" I agree. I look back at the beach to see Jeanie watching the surfer, too.

As the surfer picks up her board and starts to walk away, Jeanie hurries to catch up. Maybe Jeanie will solve the surfer mystery. I wish someone could solve my surfing problems.

Riding Waves

Sarah and I are the first to the shack the next day. Jeanie smiles when she sees us.

"I have a surprise," she says. "I found your mystery surfer, and she'll be teaching you tomorrow!"

"Who is it?" I practically yell. "Tell us! Please, Jeanie?"

"Carmen, that would ruin the surprise!" Jeanie laughs. "You'll just have to wait. For now, let's talk about how to pick waves."

Jeanie points to the water. "Waves come in groups," she explains. "The last one is usually the biggest. Don't pick the biggest one until you have lots of practice."

Sarah, of course, has no problem and even manages to surf on a small wave.

"How do you do that?" I ask. I just fell off my board again. I am getting so frustrated!

"I don't know. I just do it," says Sarah.

"Well, next to you, I look really bad," I say grumpily. "Thanks a lot."

Sarah looks sad. "I'm sorry, Carmen," she says quietly.

"No, I'm sorry, Sarah," I say. "It's not your fault. I'm just having so much trouble with this. I'm not used to being bad at sports. But so far, I only surf online."

Sarah laughs at my joke. "You're doing fine," she says. "Come on. Try again."

We begin paddling and sit up on our boards. Before I know it, Sarah is heading toward a wave. I head out after her.

I pick out a small wave and make up my mind to ride it. I only make it a few seconds before I fall, and I am back in the water.

"Do it again, Carmen!" I hear Jeanie yell.

"You did it, Carmen!" Sarah says.

I didn't feel like I was surfing. But if Jeanie and Sarah say I was, I want to try again.

Sarah and I practice for the rest of the afternoon, long after our lesson is done. After a while, I hear Jeanie calling to us from the beach.

"Carmen! Sarah! It's time to come in for dinner!" she yells.

I'm not ready to head in. I want to keep practicing.

"Bummer, dude," I say to Sarah in my best surfer voice.

"Totally," agrees Sarah. I sigh and start to paddle very slowly back to shore.

Surfing may not be my super skill, but it is starting to be a lot of fun. And we get to meet the mystery surfer tomorrow!

At lessons the next morning, a tall girl is standing with Jeannie. "Girls, this is Evie Miller," Jeanie says.

We know who Evie Miller is! She went to Victory about five years ago. And she's one of the best surfers in the world!

Jeanie points to Sarah and me. "Evie," she says. "Those two over there have been very curious about you."

"What are you doing here?" I ask.

"I'm training for a competition," Evie says.

Jeanie continues, "I know you all know who Evie is. She'll be helping us today." We all cheer.

As we start working, I hear Evie giving pointers to the other girls.

"Don't forget to bend your knees," she says. I tell myself to do the same. Soon, though, my head is swimming with so much advice that . . . *SPLASH!* I'm back in the water again.

But I am determined not to embarrass myself in front of Evie. I take a deep breath and start looking for another wave.

"Hey, Carmen!" Evie shouts from the beach. "Come here!"

I make my way toward the shore. I am ready for the break.

Evie helps me with my board. "I wanted to chat for a minute," she says. "Jeanie tells me you've been bummed about surfing."

"Oh, um, yeah. A little," I say. I didn't think Jeanie noticed.

"I get it," Evie says. "I remember camp. And I'll tell you something a lot of people don't know."

I can't believe Evie is telling me a secret!

"I went to Victory because my super skill was tennis serving," Evie says. Then she laughs at the look on my face. "I learned to surf here at camp, and I loved it. But it's not my super skill."

"But you're the best!" I say. "I don't understand."

"I just practice. Actually, I practice *a lot*," Evie says.

"But . . ." I start again. I am so surprised by Evie's secret that I can't talk!

Evie laughs again. "Carmen, do you like anything other than basketball?" she asks.

"Yeah!" I say. "I really like soccer, and I love dancing."

"And are you good at soccer and dancing?" Evie asks.

"I'm all right, I guess," I say.

Evie says, "But those aren't your super skills, right?"

"Riiiight . . ." I say slowly.

"So you practice to get good at the things you love, right? And the more you practice, the better you get. Then you love them even more, right?" Evie asks.

Now I understand! "Totally right, Evie!" I say. Evie smiles and gives me a small hug.

"Come back after lunch for another lesson," she says.

I can't wait to tell Sarah!

CHAPTER 5

I'm Surfing!

"Make sure you lean forward," Evie says when I fall off my surfboard again.

"Huh?" I ask. The water got in my ears this time.

"It's not like basketball," Evie says. "If you don't lean forward, you'll fall off backward."

I have been falling off backward a lot. I shake more water out of my ears and get back on my surfboard. I wait for a good wave and paddle out again.

This time, I will not fall off. Instead of worrying about falling, I focus on what Jeanie and Evie have told me.

I paddle out and ease up onto my feet. I bend my knees and stay bent over. That part is hard to remember. It's not like basketball at all! I spread my arms and look up at the ocean.

I'm surfing!

"Wow!" I whisper to myself. I'm smiling so big that my cheeks hurt. The wave I'm riding isn't very big, but it carries me most of the way to the beach.

Evie meets me there. Jeanie runs out from the shack with Sarah. They're all cheering for me.

"Way to go, Carmen!" Evie cheers. "I knew you could do it!"

"You were *so* right, Evie," I say. "I *love* surfing!"

"That was awesome, Carmen," says Jeanie. "I'm really proud of you!"

"Thanks, Jeanie. And thanks for sticking with me, Sarah," I say.

I did it. Everyone was right. I just needed practice. And some good advice.

GLOSSARY

defense (DEE-fens)—the team that does not have control of the ball

determined (di-TUR-mihnd)—if you are determined to do something, you have made a firm decision to do it

dribbling (DRIB-uhl-ing)—in basketball, bouncing the ball while running, keeping it under control

embarrass (em-BARE-ruhss)—if something embarrasses you, it makes you feel awkward or uncomfortable

frustrated (FRUHSS-trate-ed)—dissappointed or helpless

grumpily (GRUHM-pih-lee)—in a way that seems grouchy or cross

instructor (in-STRUHK-tor)—teacher

monstrous (MON-struhss)—huge

resort (ri-ZORT)—a place where people go for rest and relaxation

ABOUT THE AUTHOR

VAL PRIEBE

Val Priebe lives in St. Paul, Minnesota, with her four dogs, a cat named Cowboy, and a guy named Nick. When she's not writing, she enjoys coaching basketball, running, knitting, and trying out new recipes. Val is also the author of *It's Hard to Dribble with Your Feet* and *Five Fouls and You're Out* from the Victory School Superstars series.

ABOUT THE ILLUSTRATOR

JORGE SANTILLAN

Jorge Santillan got his start illustrating in the children's sections of local newspapers. He opened his own illustration studio in 2005. His creative team specializes in books, comics, and children's magazines. Jorge lives in Mendoza, Argentina, with his wife, Bety; son, Luca; and their four dogs, Fito, Caro, Angie, and Sammy.

SURFING IN HISTORY

 1779 British explorers write about Polynesians in Hawaii surfing on "belly boards."

 1820 Christian missionaries in Hawaii put limits on surfing. Yet, surfing goes on to become an important part of Hawaiian culture.

 1866 Famous author Mark Twain travels to Hawaii and tries surfing. He writes that it was a "failure."

 1912 Hawaiian Duke Kahanamoku does surfing demonstrations in southern California.

 1959 The hit movie *Gidget* features surfing, making it more popular than ever.

 1962 The Beach Boys first album *Surfin' Safari* comes out. The band and others like it help make surfing popular.

 1983 Roger Mansfield opens one of the first surf schools.

 2003 13-year-old Bethany Hamilton loses her arm when a shark attacks her while surfing. Her story is told in the 2011 movie *Soul Surfer*.

2010 Surfing's most successful competitor of all-time, Kelly Slater, is honored by the U.S. House of Representatives for his achievements.

Carmen Skore
Can't Be
Stopped!

If you liked Carmen's surfing adventure, check out her other sports stories.

It's Hard to Dribble with Your Feet

Carmen is a star basketball dribbler. But when she plays soccer, handling the ball isn't as easy. Now girls are talking about her, and she feels awful. She just didn't know that it's hard to dribble with your feet.

Five Fouls and You're Out!

When it comes to dribbling, Carmen shines on the basketball court. But on defense, she keeps racking up fouls. If she doesn't stop fouling, every game will end the same — five fouls and she's out!

THE FUN DOESN'T STOP HERE!

Discover more at . . .

www.CAPSTONEKIDS.com

- Videos & Contests
- Games & Puzzles
- Heroes & Villains
- Authors & Illustrators

Find cool websites and more books like this one at www.Facthound.com. Just type in the Book ID: 9781434222336 and you're ready to go!

AND FOR SPORTS HEADLINES, SCORES, STATS, PHOTOS, COOL GAMES . . .

SIKIDS.com